Ready to Dream

Donna Jo Napoli and Elena Furrow
illustrated by Bronwyn Bancroft

BLOOMSBURY
CHILDREN'S
BOOKS

New York • Berlin • London

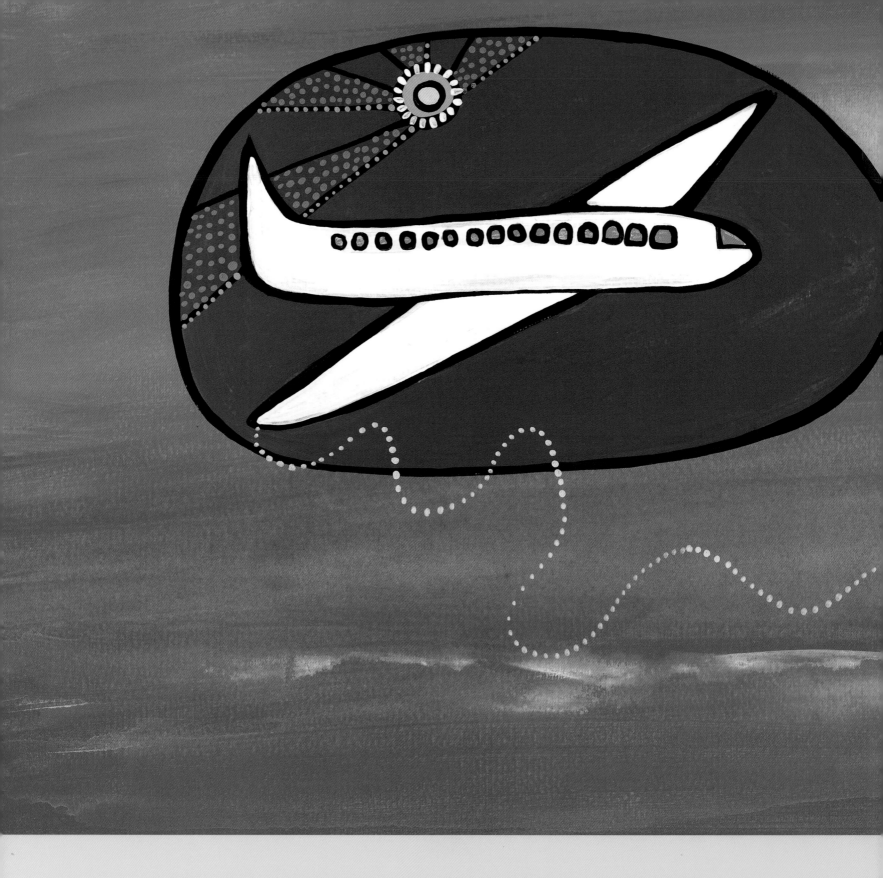

Ally jumped along as they boarded the plane. Mamma was taking her all the way to Australia.

She held her backpack tight. Inside it, her crayons, colored pencils, paints, brushes, and lots of paper were safely tucked.

The airplane ride took a day and a night.

Ally drew the ocean and the clouds.

Alice Springs, a town in the center of Australia, would be their home for a whole month. When they arrived, Ally told their taxi driver she was an artist. He pointed to an old woman on a bench and said she was an artist too.

"Can I go talk to her?" Ally asked Mamma.
"Sure, but don't be a bother."

Ally smiled at the woman.
"We flew here in a plane. Want to see?"

The woman looked at Ally's picture for a long time.

"I like the brown clouds."

"That was an accident. The plane shook and messed it up."

The woman reached down, scooped a handful of brown sand, and poured it into Ally's palm.

"When a storm blows sand into the sky, the earth dreams brown."

Sand whirled in the air and burned Ally's eyes. Was she in a sandstorm?

"My name's Ally. What's yours?"

"Pauline."

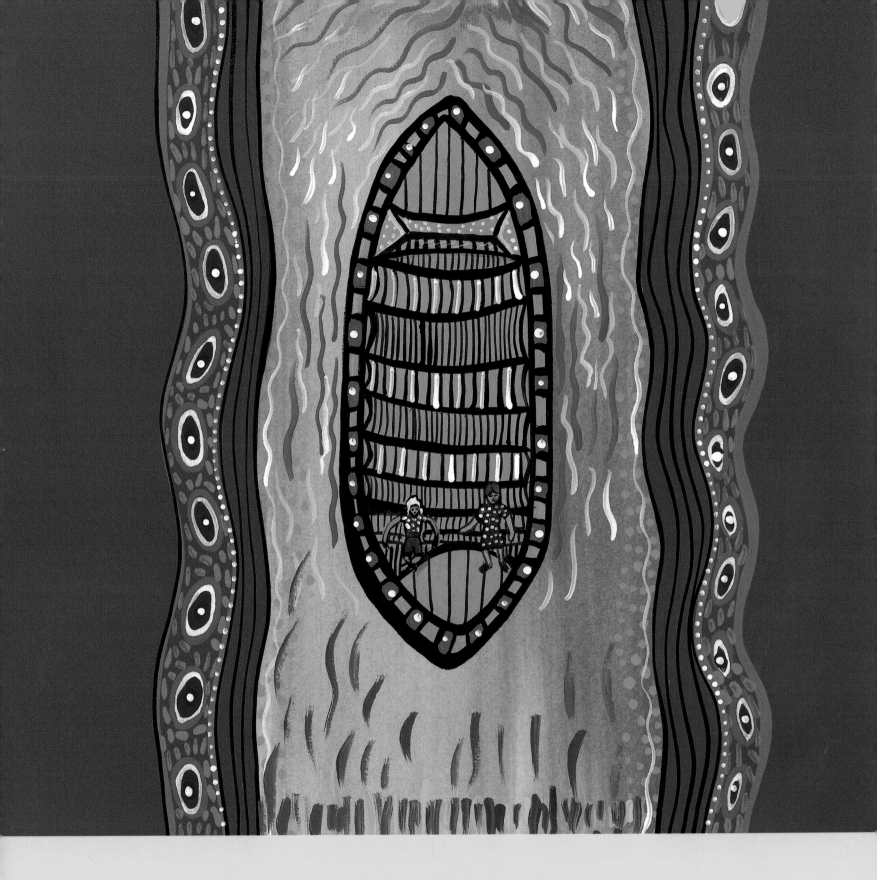

That week Mamma and Ally took a riverboat up north. Ally wanted to use brown sand instead of paint for color.

All she found was gray mud, but the sunlight made her pictures glisten.

Back in Alice Springs, Ally saw Pauline again.

"I saw fruit bats," Ally said. "And dingoes. And crocodiles."

Pauline touched the corner of the picture. "Nice ragged edge."

Ally wrinkled her nose. "It got caught on the zipper of my backpack."

"Crocodiles dream strong; their teeth chomp and tear. Maybe you should bite off the other three corners."

Ally tapped her fingertip on that ripped corner.

Ouch. Did it give her a nip?

The next week Ally and Mamma took a trip to the desert.

Ally looked for something strong to paint on—something as strong as crocodile teeth.

When they returned, Ally found Pauline walking along the roadside.

"I saw galahs and a bandicoot and kangaroos." She took a rock out of her pocket and handed it to Pauline. "That's a kangaroo. I painted other rocks too, but they fell through a hole in my backpack and bounced all the way down a ravine. They're lost."

"Down a ravine? That's good. Kangaroos dream free." Pauline gave back the rock.

"Throw this furry one, so he can hop free too."

The rock seemed to jump in Ally's hand. She threw it high and watched it bounce away.

Was that fur moving in the wind?

The third week Mamma took Ally on a train ride south.

This time Ally touched rocks and leaves and branches, and she gathered furry bits of eucalyptus bark.

When Ally returned, Pauline was leaning against a wall, looking out over the desert.

"I saw fairy penguins and a duck-billed platypus and koalas. See my koala?"

Pauline petted the koala. "No accidents this time?"

"No, but my painting keeps curling."

Pauline put her hands to Ally's cheeks.

"Koalas dream in warm balls in the crooks of trees. Let it curl."

Ally let go of the corners, and the bark curled up in her hands.

Was this koala sleeping?

As they drove east on their final trip of the summer, Ally looked
for something warm to paint on.

She ran to find Pauline when they got back.

"I saw wombats and opossums and rainbow lorikeets! Look!" Ally flapped her arms.

"See the lorikeet feathers?"

"Crocodiles bite, kangaroos bounce, koalas curl," said Pauline. "Every picture has a story to tell. Let the lorikeet dream its story."

Ally closed her eyes. Her arms seemed to rise on their own as she circled the tree.

Was she flying?

The next day Ally explored all on her own.
She saw a thorny devil and ants and a goanna.
She walked in a wide arc around a snake.

Then she lay on the sand and looked up as the night stars came out.

In the morning she visited Pauline. "I saw so many things."

"Did you paint them?"

"No, but I can show you."

Ally sat down and drew a giant goanna with her finger in the sand. Pauline joined her, adding dots all around.

A sudden wind came up and blew away their drawing. Ally laughed.
"Our picture's everywhere."
Pauline smiled. "...ou're ready to dream."

To Hayden, love Mamma and Nonna —E. F. and D. J. N.

To my three children, Jack, Ella, and Rubyrose: dare to dream, love Mum —B. B.

Published by Bloomsbury U.S.A. Children's Books
175 Fifth Avenue, New York, New York 10010

Library of Congress Cataloging-in-Publication Data
Napoli, Donna Jo.
Ready to dream / by Donna Jo Napoli and Elena Furrow ;
illustrated by Bronwyn Bancroft. — 1st U.S. ed.
p.   cm.
Summary: While drawing pictures of the animals she sees on her trip to Australia, a young girl
named Ally meets Pauline, an aborigine woman and fellow artist, from whom Ally learns that art
is not always created with just paper and paints, and that mistakes are actually happy accidents.
ISBN-13: 978-1-59990-049-0 • ISBN-10: 1-59990-049-1 (hardcover)
[1. Art—Fiction. 2. Artists—Fiction. 3. Creative ability—Fiction. 4. Aboriginal Australians—Fiction.
5. Animals—Australia—Fiction. 6. Animals in art—Fiction. 7. Australia—Fiction.]
I. Furrow, Elena. II. Bancroft, Bronwyn, ill. III. Title.
PZ7.N15Re 2009   [E]—dc22   2008024299

Art created with Matisse Acrylics on Canson Archival paper
Typeset in Antique Olive
Book design by Nicole Gastonguay

First U.S. Edition 2009
Printed in China
2 4 6 8 10 9 7 5 3 1